The Fox and the Stork

Based on a story by Aesop

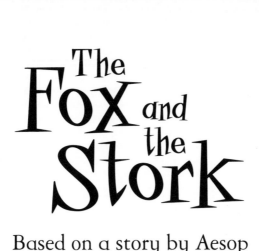

Retold by
Mairi Mackinnon

Illustrated by
Rocío Martínez

Reading Consultant: Alison Kelly
Roehampton University

Fox and Stork
were friends,

but Fox loved
playing tricks.

3

One day, he
had an idea.

He asked Stork
to dinner.

5

Stork was very hungry.

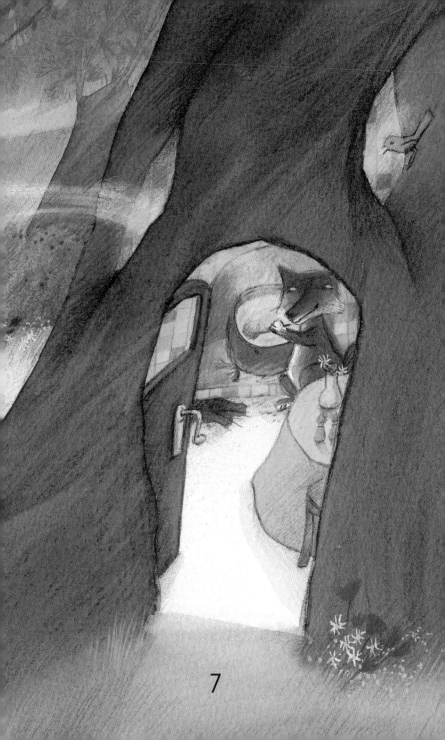

Fox poured soup
into wide bowls.

9

Poor Stork!

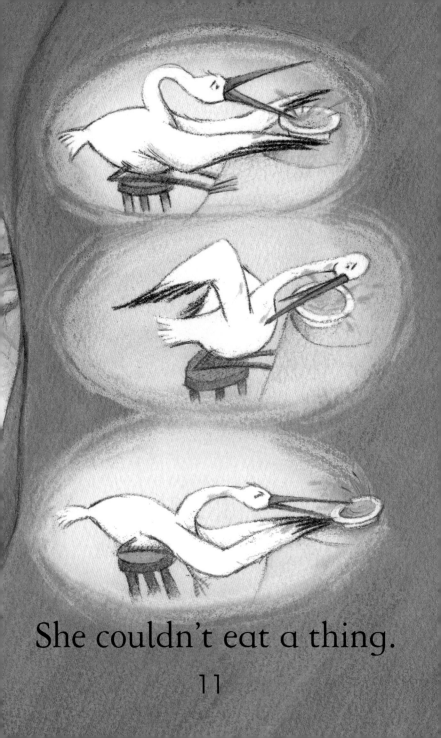

She couldn't eat a thing.

11

"Don't you like it?"
said Fox.

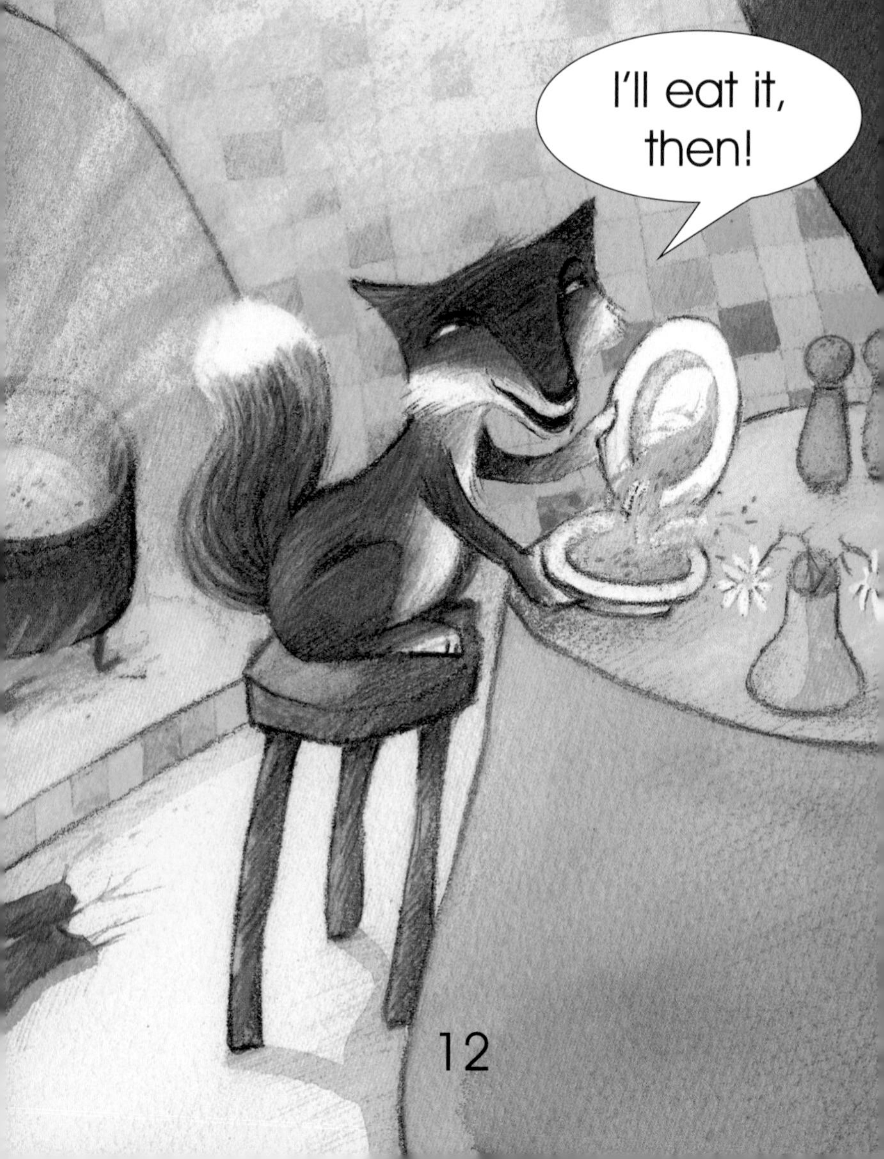

The next day, Stork
asked Fox to dinner.

Stork poured soup
into tall jars.

Poor Fox! He couldn't eat a thing.

Fox was angry.
"You tricked me!"

But Stork said,
"You tricked me first."

"Always be kind to your friends," said Stork,

"and they
will be kind
to you."

PUZZLES

Puzzle 1

Help Fox spot the differences.
There are eight to find.

Puzzle 2
How is Stork
feeling?
Match each
sentence to
a picture.

I'm not sorry.
I'm annoyed.
I'm hungry.
I'm excited.

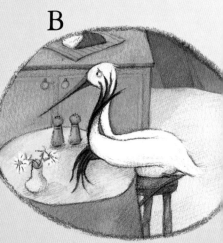

C

D

27

Puzzle 3
Choose the best sentence in each picture.

A

B

Answers to puzzles

Puzzle 1

Puzzle 2

A

I'm excited.

I'm hungry.

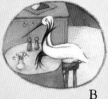

B

C

I'm annoyed.

I'm not sorry.

D

Puzzle 3

A

"Is it ready?"

C

"I can't wait!"

B

"What's the matter?"

D

"It's your fault."

About the story

The Fox and the Stork is one of Aesop's Fables, a collection of stories first told in Ancient Greece around 4,000 years ago. The stories always have a "moral" (a message or lesson) at the end.

Series editor: Lesley Sims

Designed by Non Figg

First published in 2007 by Usborne Publishing Ltd., Usborne House,
83-85 Saffron Hill, London EC1N 8RT, England. www.usborne.com
Copyright © 2007 Usborne Publishing Ltd.